FRANKLIN PARK PUBLIC LIBRARY

3 1316 00367 4010

W9-AXP-532

FRANKLIN PARK PUBLIC LIBRARY
FRANKLIN PARK, ILL.

Each borrower is held responsible for all library
material drawn on his card and for fines accruing on
the same. No material will be issued until such fine
has been paid.

All injuries to library material beyond reasonable
wear and all losses shall be made good to the
satisfaction of the Librarian.

**Replacement costs will be
billed after 42 days overdue.**

THE HARDY BOYS

UNDERCOVER BROTHERS™

FRANKLIN PARK LIBRARY
FRANKLIN PARK, IL.

PAPERCUTZ™

THE HARDY BOYS GRAPHIC NOVELS AVAILABLE FROM PAPERCUTZ

Graphic Novel #1
"The Ocean of Osyria"

Graphic Novel #2
"Identity Theft"

Graphic Novel #3
"Mad House"

Graphic Novel #4
"Malled"

Graphic Novel #5
"Sea You, Sea Me!"

Graphic Novel #6
"Hyde & Shriek"

Graphic Novel #7
"The Opposite Numbers..."

Graphic Novel #8
"Board To Death"

Coming in June:
Graphic Novel #9
"To Die Or Not To Die?"

$7.95 each in paperback, $12.95 each in hardcover. Please add $3.00 for postage
and handling for the first book, add $1.00 for each additional book. Please make check payable to NBM Publishing.

Send to: **Papercutz, 40 Exchange Place, Suite 1308 New York, NY 10005** • www.papercutz.com

THE HARDY BOYS ®

UNDERCOVER BROTHERS™

#8

Board To Death

SCOTT LOBDELL • Writer

PAULO HENRIQUE • Artist

Cover by DANIEL RENDON

Based on the series by
FRANKLIN W. DIXON

New York

J-GN .
HARDY BOYS
367-4010

Board To Death
SCOTT LOBDELL – Writer
PAULO HENRIQUE — Artist
MARK LERER – Letterer
LAURIE E. SMITH — Colorist
JIM SALICRUP — Editor-in-Chief

ISBN-10: 1-59707-053-X paperback edition
ISBN-13: 978-1-59707-053-9 paperback edition
ISBN-10: 1-59707-054-8 hardcover edition
ISBN-13: 978-1-59707-054-6 hardcover edition

Copyright © 2007 by Simon & Schuster, Inc.
Published by arrangement with Aladdin Paperbacks,
an imprint of Simon & Schuster Children's Publishing Division.
The Hardy Boys is a trademark of Simon
& Schuster, Inc. All rights reserved.

Printed in China

10 9 8 7 6 5 4 3 2 1

HERE...

...I GRABBED THESE FROM PINKSHADE'S TRAILER. THEY ARE HER SPARE BOARDS.

I KNOW THE RIDE IS FUN, BUT KEEP YOUR EYES OPEN.

THERE'S A KILLER DOWN HERE WITH US -- I HAVEN'T FORGOTTEN.

WE HAVE TO FIND HIM BEFORE HE DOES SOMETHING TO PINKSHADE!

FWING!

WE'LL FIND HIM. HE COULDN'T HAVE GONE FAR...

...HE STILL THINKS HE'S GOING TO ACE THIS COMPETITION!

CHAPTER NINE: "BOOM!"

PINKSHADE TOLD US WHAT HAPPENED.

WE'LL TAKE HIM FROM HERE, MR. HARDY.

THANK YOU, OFFICERS.

HEH HEH

CLAK!

YOU'RE PRETTY HAPPY FOR A GUY WHO IS GOING TO JAIL FOR A LONG TIME.

HA HA

BECAUSE I'LL HAVE MY REVENGE ON YOU AND YOUR BROTHER.

I REPLACED HIS BOARD WITH ONE MADE OF PLASTIQUE EXPLOSIVES.

BOOM!

WHEN HE LANDS AFTER HIS JUMP...?

AND YOU'RE TOO LATE TO STOP IT!

TOO LATE! HA HA HA HA!

Don't miss THE HARDY BOYS Graphic Novel # 9 – "To Die Or Not To Die?"

Announcing a
NANCY DREW
Adventure so
BIG

IT *TAKES* 3 GRAPHIC NOVELS TO *TELL THE ENTIRE STORY!*

THE HIGH MILES MYSTERY

Nancy Drew ® Simon & Schuster

Has Nancy Drew solved the energy crisis? This all-new story begins when she sets out to find a long-lost engine able to get 200 miles per gallons. There's just one problem – the engine is haunted.

Go Undercover in Paris as Nancy Drew® in
Danger by Design

You, as Nancy Drew, are in Paris to work undercover for a prestigious fashion designer. Minette is all the rage in the fashion world, but strange threats and unwelcome guests are causing her to unravel. It's up to you to stitch the clues together and unmask the mystery in this PC adventure game.

dare to play™

FOR MYSTERY FANS 10 to Adult

Nancy Drew PC Adventure Game #14
Order online at www.HerInteractive.com
or call 1-800-461-8787. Also in stores!
Compatible with WINDOWS® 98/2000/Me/XP/Vista

Created by

Copyright © 2006 Her Interactive, Inc. HER INTERACTIVE, the HER INTERACTIVE logo and DARE TO PLAY are trademarks of Her Interactive, Inc. NANCY DREW is a registered trademark of Simon & Schuster, Inc. Licensed by permission of Simon & Schuster, Inc.

NANCY DREW®

A NEW GRAPHIC NOVEL EVERY 3 MONTHS!

#1 "The Demon of River Heights"
ISBN 1-59707-000-9 pb.

#2 "Writ In Stone" ISBN 1-59707-002-5 pb.

#3 "The Haunted Dollhouse"
ISBN 1-59707-008-4 pb.

#4 "The Girl Who Wasn't There"
ISBN 1-59707-012-2 pb.

#5 "The Fake Heir" ISBN 1-59707-024-6 pb.

#6 "Mr. Cheeters Is Missing"
ISBN 1-59707-030-0 pb.

#7 "The Charmed Bracelet"
ISBN 1-59707-036-X pb.

NEW! **#8 "Global Warning"**
ISBN 1-59707-051-3 pb.

All: Pocket sized, 96pp., full color, $7.95

Also available in hardcover! $12.95 each.
Vol. 1: ISBN 1-59707-004-1
Vol. 2: ISBN 1-59707-006-8
Vol. 3: ISBN 1-59707-009-2
Vol. 4: ISBN 1-59707-013-0
Vol. 5: ISBN 1-59707-025-4
Vol. 6: ISBN 1-59707-031-9
Vol. 7: ISBN 1-59707-037-8
Vol. 8: ISBN 1-59707-052-1

Nancy Drew Boxed Set, #1-4
384 pages of color comics!
$29.95, ISBN 1-59707-038-6

ZORRO®

#1 "Scars!" ISBN 1-59707-016-5
#2 "Drownings!" 1-59707-018-1
#3 "Vultures!"
Zorro is left for the vultures to feast on after he tries to stop Lockspur from stealing Normandie Caniff's late husband's artwork!
ISBN 1-59707-020-3
Each: 5x7 1/2, 96pp., full color paperback: $7.95

Also available in hardcover!
$12.95 each.
Vol. 1: ISBN 1-59707-017-3
Vol. 2: ISBN 1-59707-019-X
Vol. 3: ISBN 1-59707-021-1

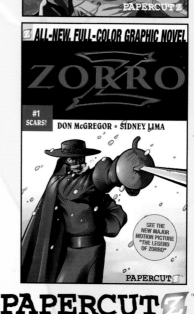

Nancy Drew ® Simon & Schuster

©2006 Zorro Productions, Inc. All Rights Reserved. ZORRO®.

PAPERCUTZ™

At your store or order at Papercutz, 40 Exchange Place, Ste. 1308, New York, NY 10005, 1-800-886-1223 (M-F 9-6 EST)

MC, VISA, AMEX accepted, add $3 P&H for 1st item, $1 each additional. Distributed by Holtzbrinck.

www.papercutz.com

THE HARDY BOYS

UNDERCOVER BROTHERS™

ATAC BRIEFING FOR AGENTS FRANK AND JOE HARDY

MISSION:

A man has been murdered, possibly over a map to a precious golden mummy. Are there other treasure-hunters trying to find the location of the tomb? Could there be a curse surrounding the ancient mummy and his treasure?

LOCATION:

Cairo, Egypt, and the surrounding area.

SUSPECTS:

Several people on an expedition are suspects. you have to find them before they find the mummy . . . and his treasure!

#13: THE MUMMY'S CURSE
Available December 2006

THIS MISSION REQUIRES YOUR IMMEDIATE ATTENTION. PICK UP A COPY OF *THE MUMMY'S CURSE* AND GET ON THE CASE!

Have you read Frank and Joe's latest stories of crime, danger, mystery, and death-defying stunts?

TOP TEN WAYS TO DIE   MARTIAL LAW   BLOWN AWAY   HURRICANE JOE   TROUBLE IN PARADISE

Visit www.SimonSaysSleuth.com for more Hardy Boys adventures.

ALADDIN PAPERBACKS • SIMON & SCHUSTER CHILDREN'S PUBLISHING

The Hardy Boys © Simon & Schuster, Inc.

WATCH OUT FOR PAPERCUT**Z**

The publisher of graphic novels created just for YOU!

Hi, Papercutz people! It's me Jim Salicrup, the luckiest graphic novel editor in the world! Every day I get to work with the best writers, artists, letterers, and colorists to create comics for the best fans in the world – YOU!

As you may've noticed, we've added these Papercutz back-pages — at no extra cost – to all of our ongoing graphic novel series. It's our way of keeping you up-to-date with all the excitement happening at Papercutz.

For example, we've got a great interview with Hardy Boys writer Scott Lobdell, an update on the new Nancy Drew movie, reports on Papercutz on Campus and in The New Book of Knowledge, and even a look at the very first Hardy Boys comicbook!

In fact, we're covering so much that we don't have any room left to tell you what's up in the world of Totally Spies! You'll just have to check www.papercutz.com or www.totallyspies.com for latest news regarding Alex, Sam, and Clover.

And don't forget – we always want to hear from you! Tell us what you think of our stories, our artwork, our characters, or anything at all regarding our graphic novels! Email me at salicrup@papercutz.com or send your comments to Papercutz, 40 Exchange Place, Ste. 1308, New York, NY 10005. Our goal is to create the kind of graphic novels that you want – so tell us how we're doing!
Thanks,

Jim

Totally Spies! is a trademark of Marathon Animation ©2006 Marathon-Mystery Animation Inc. All rights rserrved.
Caricature drawn by Steve Brodner at The 2005 MoCCA Art Fest.

97

PAPERCUT Z™
ON CAMPUS

This may be hard to believe, but once upon a time comics were actually looked down upon by certain ill-informed individuals. We're delighted to report that those dark days are far behind us. These days comics and graphic novels are now strongly embraced by the academic community. Recently Papercutz Editor-in-Chief Jim Salicrup and Zorro writer Don McGregor were

invited to join Pete Friedrich, editor of Roadstrips: A Graphic Journey Across America, on a panel hosted by Publishers Weekly Senior News Editor, Calvin Reid, all about graphic novels at the Columbia School of Journalism. The panel was presented before the one hundred students enrolled in the publishing course, which included graphic novels. The highly attentive audience had lots of great questions during the Q&A segment, and moderator Calvin Reid did an amazing job of keeping our long-winded Editor-in-Chief from going off on too many tangents. Don McGregor, whose Sabre graphic novel was one of the first to be offered to the American comics market directly in 1978, spoke enthusiastically, in his inimitable manner, about his experiences in the comics world. Jim Salicrup shared some of his experiences working with Don, especially how they approached taking the classic Zorro character and adapting it into the Papercutz graphic novel style. That style is to create the best possible graphic novels for audiences of all ages. In Zorro graphic novels #1-3, Don along with artist Sidney Lima does just that.

Both Jim and Don had a great time talking to the students, and signing copies of Zorro graphic novel #1, "Scars!" But when it was all over, Jim had to restrain himself from saying, "Class dismissed!"

©2006 Zorro Productions, Inc. All Rights Reserved. ZORRO®.

The Write Stuff

When Papercutz decided to publish the adventures of The Hardy Boys in all-new graphic novels, we never imagined we'd be able to land superstar writer Scott Lobdell, famed for his best-selling run on Marvel's The Uncanny X-Men, but somehow we did! We're thankful that Scott recently took time out of his busy movie and comics writing to answer a few questions for this interview...

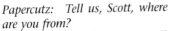

The Hardy Boys ®Simon & Schuster

Papercutz: Tell us, Scott, where are you from?
Scott: I come from a small town in upstate New York where I was raised with six brothers and sisters —quite a different experience from Joe and Frank's upbringing! I will tell you one thing, though, when you live in such a large family there isn't a lot of room for privacy so you come to appreciate your secrets because they are yours. Now, here I am, all these years later, writing the adventures of two of the world's most famous secret-busters.

Papercutz: How did you become a writer?

Scott: Years and years of rejection letters from magazines, comics, book publishers... but I kept trying. And maybe more importantly, I kept listening to the criticism and instructions from friends, family, and editors. I think, too often, beginning writers want only praise for their efforts and it is difficult to hear suggestions, or to hear that something is unclear or confusing in early drafts. I think by listening I was able to challenge myself to be a better writer. I used to say of comics "Either they are going to give up or I am! And I'm not!"

Papercutz: Did you read all the original Hardy Boys books by Franklin W. Dixon? Which is your favorite?

Scott: That is like asking me to pick out my favorite ice cream — or favorite snowflake! Every book is its own experience!

Papercutz: How would you describe the Hardy Boys?

Scott agrees with Joe and Frank: when solving crimes, two heads are better than one!

Scott: There have been a lot of famous detectives over the years, each interesting in their own way. But what I think is so compelling about Joe and Frank is their relationship. In some families there are brothers who haven't spoken for years — but here are the Hardy Boys who not only share their every adventure, but need to trust each other along every step of every case. They enjoy being together and they've always got each other's back. The only thing cooler than having a cool brother is being one.

Papercutz: Where do you get your ideas?

Scott: Specifically, my Hardy Boys ideas seem to come from the headlines. *The Ocean of Osyria* and *Identity Theft* were both based on an all too real world problems. I often think, "If Joe and Frank lived in the here and now, what kind of problems would they be called on to solve as undercover brothers?"... And then I start writing.

Papercutz: How do you like working for Papercutz?

Scott: I have known Papercutz Editor-in-Chief Jim Salicrup for... a long time! Little known fact: Jim was the editor on my first published comicbook work, the historical "Last Charlie America" story for Marvel Comics' *What The — ?! #4*! So when he complains about my rarely broken deadlines, I like to point out he has no one to blame but himself! And publisher Terry Nantier puts up with a lot but always manages to be positive and supportive.

Papercutz: How do you think Lea, Daniel, Sidney, and Paulo have handled your stories?

Scott: With that question, you've managed to stumble onto one of my favorite elements of writing this series of graphic novels. Unlike with most of my other comicbook writing, where I will write a plot for the artist and then wait for the penciled artwork before adding the dialogue, with The Hardy Boys I write a complete script – describing every scene with all the dialogue included. What is so fun about these books is that I don't even see them until they are published — so I get to experience all these talented artists and their storytelling techniques at the same time you do. Which makes me not only the writer of the Hardy Boys graphic novels... it also makes me a fan!

From left to right: Jim Salicrup, Gil Champion, Stan Lee, and Scott Lobdell.

Papercutz: What else do you write?

Scott: I am currently writing a horror movie for Rogue Pictures, a television episode of the NBC TV series, *Medium*, and an animated DVD for a guy named Ringo Starr who apparently used to be in a band from England a few years ago. (Also, if there is any justice, I'll get to work on my new favorite television show... *Jericho*!)

Papercutz: *What can you tell us about future The Hardy Boys graphic novels?*

Scott: I am very interested in seeing the brothers involved in cases that don't always come from A.T.A.C. I love this covert agency that uses the brothers to solve cases around the country — but I'd like to see Joe and Frank come across the occasional mystery in their free time.

Scott is one of the writers of Mixtionary.

The *Hardy Boys in Comics!*

Did you know that the all-new Hardy Boys graphic novels from Papercutz are not the first time Joe and Frank Hardy appeared in comics? It's actually the third series of Hardy Boys comics. We've done a little detective work ourselves and have come up with a bit of background information on the historic, very first series of Hardy Boys comics.

Way back in the 1940s and 1950s, one of the biggest comicbook publishers was Dell Comics. Known for their snappy motto, "Dell Comics are Good Comics," one of their top titles was called Four Color Comics, a reference to the four basic colors used in printing comicbooks. Surprisingly, the "Four Color Comics" title wasn't on most of its covers. According to the Official Overstreet Comic Book Price Guide, Dell published two series of Four Color Comics, the first lasting just 25 issues, and the second running for a record-breaking 1,354 issues. Yet it only was called Four Color Comics on #19 – 25 of the first series and on #1-99 and 101 of the second. Each issue featured a popular TV, movie, or comic strip character, and it was the name of the featured character that was displayed as the title on the covers. One issue could feature a western adventure based on the Gunsmoke TV series, another could adapt a John Wayne movie such as The Searchers, and yet another could spotlight comic-strip star, Mandrake, the Magician. In 1956, Four Color Comics #760 featured Walt Disney's The Hardy Boys.

"*Walt Disney's* The Hardy Boys"? That's correct. Back in 1955, the daily Disney TV series, The Mickey Mouse Club, featured a live-action four-part Hardy Boys adventure, "The Mystery of the Applegate Treasure" based on the classic Franklin W. Dixon series. The serial starred Tim Considine as Frank Hardy, Tommy Kirk as Joe Hardy, Russ Conway as Fenton Hardy, Carol Ann Campbell as Iola Morton, and Sarah Selby as Aunt Gertrude. Each episode was just fifteen minutes long, but it must've packed quite a punch. Just a couple of years later, the same cast were reunited for a fifteen-part Hardy Boys serial for The Mickey Mouse Club called "The Mystery of the Ghost Farm." The episodes have recently been released on DVD as part of the Walt Disney Treasures series.

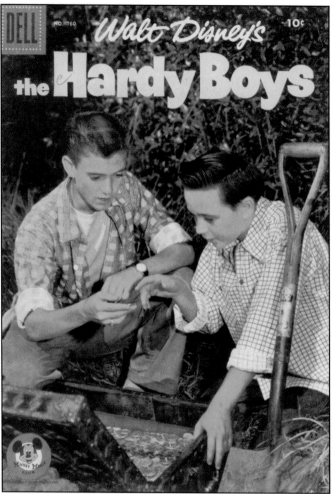

The very first Hardy Boys comicbook.

The Hardy Boys ®Simon & Schuster

Papercutz Trivia Quiz

1) Who is the other Papercutz superstar who appeared on a Disney series in the 50s?

2) Which real-life Papercutz person appeared on Disney's The Mickey Mouse Club?

(Answers on next page)

Since Four Color Comics adapted so many Disney TV shows, it seemed only natural that they'd also include the TV version of The Hardy Boys. While the stars were just 15 and 14 years old at the time of their first Hardy Boys serial, and Tommy Kirk wasn't blond, the serial did capture the spirit of the classic books. The comic-book covers featured photos from the TV serial, and the interior artwork featured the actors' likenesses. The first comic nicely adapted "The Mystery of the Applegate Treasure," with suitably shadowy artwork providing the proper mysterious mood. Three more issues of Four Color

Hardy Boys DVD

Comics featured The Hardy Boys, #830 (August '57), #887 (January '58), and #964 (January '59). The Hardy Boys wouldn't appear in comics again until 1970 – but that's a story we'll save for the next installment of "The Hardy Boys in Comics!"

Available now!

Answers:

1) The star of three Papercutz graphic novels, Zorro. He was played by Guy Williams in the Disney TV series, which debuted September, 1957.

2) Papercutz Editor-in-Chief Jim Salicrup appeared on an episode of the 90's revival of The Mickey Mouse Club, which also featured Britney Spears, Christina Aguilera, K.C. Chasez, Keri Russell, Ryan Gosling, and Justin Timberlake.

106

NANCY DREW

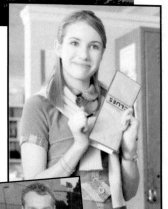

NANCY DREW MOVIE UPDATE – COMING SOONER!

Great news, Nancy Drew fans! The release of the all-new Nancy Drew movie Warner Bros. has been moved from August 2007 to June 2007! That's right, the movie we've all been waiting for will soon be at your local multiplex starting the 15th of June 2007, starring Emma Roberts, of Nickelodeon's hit show *Unfabulous*, as our favorite Girl Detective.

Time Magazine, commenting on a Emma's similarity to a certain major movie star said, "Jeepers, she looks familiar!" Noting that Emma "shares the broad, screen-ready smile of her Aunt Julia (yes, that Julia)." The New York Daily News reported that Emma thought making the film "was a lot of hard work" but that she "liked the way it turned out." In the movie she has to "unravel a Hollywood mystery. Probably the most challenging thing was there was a lot of running around and a lot of stunts." The movie also stars Tate Donovan, as Nancy's lawyer dad, Carson Drew.

SLEUTHS IN A BOX!

Nancy Drew©Simon & Schuster

Nancy Drew in a box.

Back when Nancy Drew and her friend Kalpana were trying to escape from the bad guys in Nancy Drew graphic novel #4 "The Girl Who Wasn't There," they chose to get into a wooden box. It wasn't one of the Girl Detective's better ideas – they got bounced around pretty bad before getting re-captured.

What is a good idea, however, is collecting the first four volumes of Nancy Drew's Papercutz graphic novels in a box. It's such a good idea, that the first four Hardy Boys Papercutz graphic novels are also being collected in a boxed set. If you just started reading either series, these boxed sets are a great way to catch up on the early volumes at a great price. It's also a cool way to store your Nancy Drew and Hardy Boys graphic novels on your book-shelf.

As a super special bonus, every Nancy Drew boxed set also features the Her Interactive Nancy Drew PC game "The Haunted Carousel." The game itself is sold separately for about $20.00, but comes free with the Nancy Drew boxed set. This has got to be one of the best deals ever! And since the Boxed Set also features Nancy Drew graphic novel #4, you get to see how Nancy and Kalpana finally do escape the bad guys!

Even if you already have these great graphic novels, the Nancy Drew and The Hardy Boys Boxed Sets make a great holiday or birthday present for friends or family.

If you can't find these great Papercutz Boxed Sets at your favorite bookstores, or at Target or Sam's Clubs, just ask your favorite bookstore to order it for you. They'll be happy to do it.

TWO FOR THE BOOKS...

Everyone at Papercutz is still bustin' with pride that our very first Nancy Drew graphic novel, "The Demon of River Heights" won the 2006 Ben Franklin Award for Best Graphic Novel of the year. So you can just imagine how we felt when we saw The New Book of Knowledge 2006 Annual and it featured an article about the 75th Anniversary of Nancy Drew. The Young People's Book of the Year highlights events from 2005, and right there on page 259 is the beautiful cover of Nancy Drew graphic novel # 1 drawn by Sho Murase. The article is very well-written, giving a fact-filled history of everyone's favorite Girl Detective.

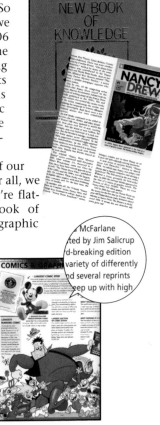

For all of us at Papercutz, the publication of our first graphic novels was a major event. After all, we were launching our company as well. We're flattered that the editors of The New Book of Knowledge included the Nancy Drew graphic novel amongst all the amazing events of 2005. We're proud to be a small part of pop culture phenomenon that is Nancy Drew.

And if all of that wasn't enough to give us all swelled heads, you should've seen our Editor-in-Chief Jim Salicrup when Papercutz letterer Mark Lerer showed him the 2007 Guinness Book of World Records. Turns out that Spider-Man #1, the comic written and drawn by Todd McFarlane that Jim launched back when he was an editor at Marvel Comics is cited as the biggest-selling single-edition issue of comic ever published. While Jim is thrilled by the recognition, he vows to break that record at Papercutz. And at the rate things have been going for the graphic novel publisher for tweens, that may not be such an impossible goal!

A PAPERCUTZ™ MINI-MYSTERY?

Can you identify the boy being shot at on this page?

©2005 Edizione Piemme S.P.A.   English language worldwide edition ©2006 by Papercutz

Turn the page for the answer...

...it's young Karol Wojtyla, the boy who would become Pope John Paul II.

It's just a small part of the special Papercutz graphic novel The Life of John Paul II ...*In Comics!* It's an epic true tale of a young Polish boy and his amazing life. Here's a review that we just have to share with you...

"Once in a lifetime, someone extraordinary rises from the sea of humanity to lead by example.

"Pope John Paul II, Karol Wojtyla, was that man for our century. The leader of the Catholic Church, he rose from war torn Poland amidst propaganda, from a life of athletics to answer the greater call. Karol Wojtyla (1920-2005) gave himself fully to the Church, his savior Jesus, and to the service of those around him.

"Alessandro Mainardi and Werner Maresta and have combined their talents to tell the story of the Man who would be Pope, the man who reached out to the youth of the world, the man who reached out with an olive branch of ecumenism. The resulting 96 page graphic novel is outstanding. With such an active life, this could easily have been a thousand-pages long, but prayerfully chosen incidents portray the growth of young Karol from child, to actor, to priest, to bishop to Pope. Along the way, God's hand can be clearly seen in his life. As Pope, he traveled the world. As Pope, he reached out to any who hear. As Pope, he visited his native Poland to bring the gospel message and hope.

"The inspirational papacy he led is described from his own words and his faith and hope clearly shine through. I love the inclusion of scripture, and the thoughtful pacing of the story. Even after his passing, his influence will carry on.

"One of the many faith filled moments that captured me as I read this was the closing of his letters...OAMG, 'Omnium ad Maioram Dei Gloriam', all in the highest glory of God. I was filled with awe and a sense of admiration for Pope John Paul II.

"Through his example, the whole world was inspired. Just like you will be when you read this book.

"Look for this at your local bookstore or online at www.papercutz.com.

"I remain,

"A man of faith.

"Tim Lasiuta

"OAMG"